Dedica

Thank you for

And showing me the true meaning to being strong.

I miss you.

1

Well today's the day, she thought. Anything has got to be better for me than this. Today was the day Cecilia left the place she's called home all her adult life and goes to live with her friends in California.

It'll be nice she thought as she was getting dressed in her room. Aunt Kat was taking her to the airport, and her friends were picking her up to start her new life. It shouldn't be so bad I mean I grew up there, she thought, so why do I have such a bad feeling?

She kept going through the motions of the morning it's only four am, by the time she gets to California it will be around three in the afternoon. "Hey sweetie I know you're scared to leave," said aunt Kat "but trust me, this is what your mother would've wanted. Ya know there's nothing really here for you anymore, and I know how much you loved California when you would visit your friends and" oh no, Cecilia thought. It's another rant "don't be silly , aunt Kat, as long as you're here there will always be something here for me."

With that they headed out to the airport, nothing fancy just your typical small town thing she thought. She was staring out the window thinking of her mom, and how she would laugh and it made the world brighter, or how her hair, the color of the sandy brown shores of the beach, would be braided or tied behind her head in perfect intricate ways. She would always remember her mom as she had been in life not as she had been at the viewing, then she'd looked like a wax doll. Never once a live, breathing person but a doll made to just lie there and resemble that of her mother.

When she turned to her aunt she realized that she had asked her a question. "Are you still with me honey? I know it's hard because you've come to love it here ever since your mom and dad split when you were twelve but California's not that bad." She left it at that, and Cecilia tried to muster a smile but it didn't feel real, it felt forced and almost painful.

When they got to the airport Cecilia didn't know whether to feel happy or sad. She was happy to finally be doing something, putting this behind her, and moving on. But she was sad, of course, to be leaving her home and her aunt. What if Aunt Kats not as ok as she seems? She thought, what if she's like me, depending on anything and everything to take her mind off of her pain and sadness? Her aunt turned and said " well sweety you better get going, before they leave without you. Did you get in touch with your friends?" She smiled but Cecilia could tell she was trying to hold herself together until she was alone. So hastily Cecilia said"yes of course, they're going to come to the airport and pick me up. We talked last night everything's worked out."

They hugged one last time both trying as hard as they could to not cry in front of the other. She walked through the baggage check-in and finally got to her gate. When the plane finally boarded, she felt a small sense of fear at leaving everything she knew for nothing she's known since she was a kid. She put her headphones in and leaned against the window hoping to get a little sleep before seeing everyone.

As she started to drift she heard someone talking she realized it was the person beside her. When she went to answer she realized they were on the phone ugh people I swear she thought. Then she drifted off to a well deserved sleep for most of the flight.

2

When she woke it was to a flight attendant gently shaking her awake telling her they've landed in San Diego. She blinked a few times and got her bearings ok, she thought, I'm here. They're going to pick me up and everything's going to be ok. When she got off the plane with her carry-on, and had her bags from baggage claim, she walked out to the entrance to find her friends.

At first she didn't see them, last time she'd seen them in person had been six years ago when they were all twelve. Now, at eighteen -and knowing each other through pictures, texts, Face-Time, and any other form of technology- she wasn't sure how exactly she'd find them. Oh god she thought what if they're not here? And I'm just stuck waiting?

Just as she started to panic, she heard someone call her name loudly. She turned and saw a tall blonde/brunette girl in leggings and a black shirt with a snowman? Was it holding knives? And tennis shoes wave at her and run towards her. Behind her was another girl but this one had darker brunette hair was in a green shirt and black shorts waving from afar and staying firmly in place.

When the first one got to her they hugged and laughed and almost started crying "oh my gosh Kimberly it's been so long." Said Cecilia "I hadn't realized how much you and your sister have changed!" The girl, Kimberly, stood back a few feet and looked her up and down finally she said "me? I've changed? honey you have black hair now and you're wearing actual clothes when we were kids I was lucky to get you out of pjs." We both laughed and started walking towards her sister. "Ok Ceci, so you know me" said Kimberly, "and obviously you know Melanie" she said indicating the other girl. She smiled and waved "but this, this is one of our friends he was bored and decided to come to the airport with us. His names Ryan. He kind of lives with us."

When Cecilia looked up she saw a tall boy standing there wow, he's gotta be like 6'2 she thought, he had brown spiky hair, blue green eyes that were curious looking, a perfect face, and along with that Cecilia saw a perfect body. He held his hand out and said "hi I'm Ryan, as I'm uh sure you heard. I moved here from Michigan a few years back." She smiled and shook his hand he seemed nice she thought.

"Well let's get this train rolling guys." Kimberly went to help grab a couple bags but Ryan moved before she could get them and carried them out to the car. "So how did you guys meet and become roommates?" Cecilia had been dying to ask and it just slipped out. Her friend stopped a minute and giggled a little " oh Ceci, not even five minutes and you are on that boys case. I knew bringing him was a good idea. I met him at school we had a ton of classes together junior and senior year we started talking and when school was out Melanie and I scraped up our nickels and dimes and got an apartment. He was kicked out on account of 'not doing anything with his life' and asked to move in. He's pretty great, he cooks, cleans and helps with bills. We didn't ever really ask him to do it he just really likes to, cooking is his thing apparently. And besides, who would turn down a good looking guy cooking and cleaning and helping to pay bills? Not I said the fly." Ceci laughed and said "not me said the flea."

They made their way out and in to the car finally, and Ryan was in the drivers seat "what took so long?" Kimberly laughed and said "oh ya know, just enjoying the view."

With that, he shrugged and looked at Melanie in the rearview mirror and smiled. "Alright ladies I guess we're off. Seat belts I'd hate to take off without a fully secured cabin." He turned to the passenger seat and looked pointedly at Kimberly who was taking a selfie with Ceci. "What?" She asked "hey, I haven't seen her in six years. Yes we're going to take a selfie calm yourself." With that, she grumbled and put her seatbelt on while Ceci covered a laugh with a cough.

The ride to the house was quiet and pleasant Ceci thought. As they pulled up she noticed first it was really nice, a little too nice for people who had to scrape up their nickels and dimes, and second that it had crosses above the entryway on the outside and inside.

Ceci frowned a little I don't remember them ever being religious, she thought. Oh well something to ask about later.

She went back to the truck to help get her things and heard a thud like somebody falling over. When she looked she saw Ryan had thrown one of her bags at Kimberly and it had taken her by surprise and knocked her off her feet. She stood up and flared slightly at Ryan. "Fine do it by yourself Mr. I'm-so -perfect. I'll just give Ceci a tour."

When Ceci turned and looked for Melanie she found she couldn't see her. "Where's your sister?" Kim frowned a little "eh she never helps with hard labor, she's probably up in her room. She doesn't really come out much so....."

The way she let the sentence hang between them as a yea-don't-really-bug-her-and-she-won't,-or-shouldn't,-bug-you. Ceci smiled and nodded looking toward the house "this house is amazing Kim. How did you guys afford it? You said you scraped your nickels and dimes together for an apartment this is like a lot of nickels and dimes."

Kim nodded and thought about it as they stood on the porch it was an older house Cecilia noticed, older than most other houses in the neighborhood. It reminded her of the old plantation houses back home in Louisiana. "How did you guys find a plantation home? Out here in California?" Again Kim hesitated but finally she answered "honestly, Melanie and I barely had enough for an apartment we were going to lose it,but Ryan came along and he helped pay rent there. Eventually he got a job or something and now we live here. He mostly pays for it, like we help a lot but he has it."

She looked down as if she were ashamed and when she looked up she looked sad. "Whoa, hey I'm sorry Kim I didn't mean to hurt you, so he helps you pay bills you told me before that you guys took him in for a while even when you couldn't really afford it yourself.. So he's just trying to repay you guys." With that Kim smiled and Ryan came up saying "alright tonight I'm cooking in honor of the new house guest. So I'm thinking I don't know, Chinese?" Kim laughed and said "sounds good she loves sushi? I think that's Chinese?" Then she looked at Cecilia "well how about I give you the grand tour and show you your room?"

3

'Last night was pretty nice actually, 'Cecilia wrote in her diary. 'when Ryan was done cooking they all sat down to dinner which was sushi and Chinese food all I could eat. The only weird thing though, was that Melanie never showed up to dinner she stayed in her room and when Kim went to get her Ryan stared at his plate with a look of almost disgust on his face.....

What was with that? I wasn't sure if that was actually the look but when i went to ask Kim came back down with a look of sadness on her face. Oh well I guess it's Time to get up and get my bearings here Kim said she and I can go shopping today.'

With that, Cecilia shut her diary and smiled she had on a summer dress her mom had bought her a couple years ago. I miss you mom she thought but she grabbed her shoes and headed out the door and into the bathroom to finish getting ready for the day, when she ran into Ryan. He was shirtless and in checkered black and grey pajama pants.

He stopped and looked at her in surprise and she noticed his eyes had a purplish tint to them. "What's going on with your eyes are they conta-" before she could finish her sentence Ryan turned and half walked half ran down the hall and up to the stairs that led to the attic room. She followed him and when he saw her he practically glided up the stairs and pulled them up and away from her so she couldn't follow. She stood there staring at the square in the roof when Kim came up behind her.

"Uh hey Ceci, what are you doing just standing and staring at the roof?"

Ceci jumped a little not having heard her come up "jeez what did you do float up here?" At the look on Kim's face Ceci thawed "I'm sorry Kim I was just wondering what's up with Ryan? He had these like purple contacts in and when I went to ask about it he took off up the stairs and pulled them up so I can't go." When Ceci looked at Kim she noticed that the other girl had gone completely calm and looked like nothing could bother her.

"Hmm you know I don't know Ceci, I'll ask him later" as she said the last word she looked up at the square in the roof where Ryan's room was, as if he could hear her through it. Now she looked at Ceci "well come on the mall isn't good to wait for us!" She grabbed Ceci's hand and pulled her down the stairs like the good ol days Ceci thought.

When they got out of the house and headed to the garage, which was a separate building from the house itself, Ceci stopped for a second and stared. "Is this your car Kim?"

It wasn't the best car in the entire world-nothing like a Lamborghini or convertible-but it was nice and exactly what Kim had always wanted. It was a grey Jeep Wrangler rubicon and it was nice. Raised a little even, leather seats and she even had the option to make it a convertible. "That is amazing Kim, I love it!" Ceci smiled as she jumped up into the passenger seat.

"So, where are we going I haven't been here in so long I bet everything's changed I can't wait for that sunny California weather." Kim snorted from her seat and it seemed she was trying to stop a laugh from coming out. "Oh what's so funny kim?" She didn't answer for a moment as if actually contemplating what were funny then sighed and said "nothing Ceci, besides there's a hurricane off the coast it's been nothing but clouds and cold for months now." She said "nothing we can do about it though, so looks like you're not gonna get that tan you wanted."

Ceci looked at her pale legs and felt a little sadness and that cold creep back into her for a moment. That cold that never went away since her mothers death, it was always there if she didn't feel it right at a moment she knew it was just waiting for her to drop her guard like she had, to seep back in.

She looked over and saw the other girl staring at her she realized she'd been quiet for too long. "Sorry, so what's this hurricane called where's it come from that it's so cold?" Kim, seeing her friend was ok smiled and said "well actually, it's from Alaska and it's named Ryan... We've been getting pretty sick lightning storms too. There's heat lightning that's beautiful pinks and purples oh see! There's some."

Ceci looked to where Kim had pointed out the dashboard at. She waited a moment and just like that she saw it but it wasn't the lightning or the afternoon sky she saw anymore. For a second she was back in the hallway running into Ryan and looking up to see...... Eyes, those purple, questioning almost angry eyes looking at her. But that's impossible isn't it? This is the sky and that, well that with Ryan was just a trick of light she told herself.

But why had he gotten so mad and ran from her like that? She got so caught up in her thoughts that Kim completely scared her when she touched her shoulder shaking her gently.

"Ceci? Hello earth to Cecilia? Are you ok in there?" Ceci blinked and smiled at her "sorry I guess I'm still tired." Kim shrugged and got out, when Ceci got out of the car she saw Kim on the phone and started fiddling with her bag. "Ugh bad news girl." Kim said "apparently Ryan-the-scumbag has gotten himself into trouble, so looks like I'm going to drop you off at the house and pick him up. We can go shopping another time ok?"

When they got back to the house the weather had changed dramatically, it went from just a grey lazy day to a full blown thunderstorm. The rain was pounding down on them consistently. When they got to the house there was a police car parked outside and two big suv's with completely tinted out windows. "Shit" Kimberly said " I forgot about them apparently later came sooner.. Ok, um Ceci I need you to stay in the car and duck down as far as you can. If anyone comes to the car-even a police man in uniform- do not look at him don't move."

Ceci looked at her like she was crazy but at the firm insistent look on Kim's face she knew something was wrong. "Ok Kim but one question: if I'm kneeling on the floor how will I know if it's a cop or anyone?" She smiled a sad almost wistful smile "because I won't come to that side I'll go straight to the drivers side. Only get out for me, Melanie, or Ryan ok? Now lock the doors as soon as I get out."

When Kim got out it was loud for a moment and then the door shut and it was completely quiet. Cecilia sat there for what felt like hours. She heard a weird noise just then, like metal being forcibly bent. She tried to look but for some reason she couldn't force herself to. She heard yelling and then there was something big moving by the car or even a lot of somethigs. They pushed the car this way and that Ceci tried to stay safe where she was but she was being moved all around the cars front.

When it finally stopped she heard someone shouting. It sounded almost like Kim she thought and if it was, Kim was angry. The drivers door opened and Kim was looking at her concern written all over her face.

"I think you and I need to talk Ceci." Was all she said.

4

When Cecilia was finally able to crawl out of the drivers side, the passenger side was completely smashed in, like it had been T-boned. "You better be able to fix that Ryan, or I swear you will regret it." Was all the other girl said about the car, despite several hundred questions thrown at her from Ceci.

When they got inside, she saw Melanie head up the stairs she had mud all over the bottom of her pants and caked on her shoes. But how or why? Thought Ceci, she wasn't even outside or at least I didn't see her. Kim saw her staring at Melanie and smiled a little.

"Ok so, this town has changed since you lived here.... I mean it's gotten bigger and all that obviously but it's changed in another way too." She sounded nervous and kept looking at the door as if staring at it would get Ryan or someone to walk in and help her fumble through this. "Ok, so the towns bigger that's not so hard to believe" said Ceci. After staring at the door for a minute longer Kim dropped her head and took a deep breath. When she looked up she had a resolved look on her face.

"Ok so obviously I'm alone on this one. Since you've left there have been changes that have taken place here. Which normally, you think 'well yea duh there's gonna be I've been gone for what? six years?' Ok. But no I mean big changes. About three years ago, when I was fifteen these people came one big family. Ok cool we were all happy they were from overseas so they were like absolutely gorgeous and ya know foreign.

So they threw this big party after being here for a few weeks and at the party they said some....... Pretty weird stuff." She said the last part slowly as if she didn't want to say it at all hating to have to admit it. Ceci leaned back and smiled at her hoping to encourage her to keep going. After a minute she continued " so they were talking about hierarchy and monarchy and aristocrats and all that- I didn't know what they were talking about, I was focused on one of the sons. Don't look at me like that he was gorgeous! If I'd have just known what they were talking about I would've been out of there so fast. But, I didn't I was too focused on him.

He led me outside to the backyard, which was absolutely beautiful by the way, and we went to a little sitting area." She was speaking as though this memory absolutely angered and disgusted her and she was so ashamed of herself like she hated herself Ceci thought.

When she finally started to speak again she couldn't look at Ceci she was looking everywhere around the room "it had been a cold night, that night and we were sitting outside and he was kissing me it was getting very intimate. He was telling me things and whispering in my ear, telling me everything he wanted, then he told me he wanted me to join him and his family I could rule with him. I just figured 'ok maybe he's had one too many to drink he doesn't really mean it'. So to not break the moment I smiled and agreed with him he looked me in the eyes and everything changed. The night had gone from a little chilly to bone-numbing cold. When he looked at me all the warmth had mostly gone from his eyes, and he asked me if I really meant it. Either way I wouldn't be the same the next day.

I was getting scared now and told him I wanted to go back but he grabbed me and pulled me hard. He pulled me to him and grabbed my hair with one hand and ripped my head to the side exposing my neck. He smiled and said 'what's wrong señorita? Not a moment ago you were pledging yourself to me and now you're scared?' I wasn't just scared I was absolutely frightened, freaked out, I wanted to run but when I looked at him everything went away from me I couldn't move, I couldn't call for help, I just couldn't. He kissed my jawline and down to my neck where he smiled and I thought he was going to rape me. I was so scared and he said something that frightened me even more he said 'poor señorita doesn't know that the fear rolling off of her in waves is what's feeding my bloodlust making me want her more.'"

She stopped and Ceci realized for the first time that there were tears running down the other girls face and she was trembling. "Kim I get it he was a creep you don't have to ke-" but Kim cut her off with her hand up, she took a deep breath and continued "sorry it's just I've never told anyone except Ryan and Melanie this. So, he bent down and when he went to my neck this time, he bit me." When she saw the bewildered look on Cecelia's face she nodded and pulled the neck of her sweater down revealing two marks and veins that were spiderwebbing around the area.

"Oh my god!" Said Ceci "what the hell is that Kim? You said it happened three years ago? Those look fresh!" Kim nodded and said " I'll get to that, anyway he bit me and it hurt, like I felt I was burning from the inside out everything was in pain. I was crying uncontrollably by then and he was laughing I felt my blood coming out and I started to panic I was getting weaker and weaker. He stopped and said 'señorita if I'd known Americans truly had it so good, I would've come over much sooner. If you stop struggling it won't hurt as much.' Then he went and took more.

After what felt like hours of excruciating pain, someone came back. When I looked I noticed there were black spots at the edges of my vision and it was hard to speak, I was so weak I heard someone talking and arguing then the boy, Jasper was his name, pulled out from my neck and it felt like something was ripped from my body some piece of me that would never be mine again. In the end I found out that I had not only sworn myself to him but that he now owned me body and soul to use as he wanted or needed.

After that his family took over and there was more and more of their friends coming to town. They were vampyres. I know it sounds cheesy but I mean you saw my neck, you know it's real. They've taken the town, they control it, they take who they want when they want, it doesn't matter."

Ceci sat there for a minute sitting and staring at the floor thinking of everything she had just heard the awful truth of it in Kimberly's eyes, if it's so bad she thought why stay? Why not just leave?

"I know what you're thinking, if it's bad why not leave why stay? Am I right?" Ceci looked up and saw a sad smile forming on the other girls lips "because we can't leave, anyone who lives here had to go through them to leave. If they don't think it's a good idea they don't let you. If you try to leave without them knowing, they kill you and all of your family to make sure no one else turns out like you. How did I know what you were thinking? Because the more times your ugh master" she said he word like it was poison and spit it out " takes from you, willing or not, the more you become like one you can't be a full one but you get some characteristics. The more lives you consume though the more power you get. That's why the weathers all bad, that's why we all know what to say, when to say it, how to help you.... Because we're all at the point."

A question popped in Cecilia's head " wait so you're telling me you, Melanie, and Ryan are all feeders? Or food or whatever?" Kim looked at her and chuckled a little almost as if to herself even, but she said "no, Ryan and Melanie aren't feeders they're. Well they're uh-" but Ceci got the idea "oh my god they're vampyres too!" She started breathing faster now "how can you live with them after what happened to you? What's wrong with you how could you-" but just then Ryan walked in with Melanie behind him carrying what looked like a stake and she was smiling.

Kim ducked and backed away a little so Ryan could take over "yes we're vampyres, yes Jasper took her blood three years ago, and has every other day since, but no, were not like him. We actually care about her and drink little donation bag... Things." At the look on Cecilia's face he smiled and looked at Melanie for help. She rolled her eyes and said "look facts are: Jaspers a douche, his family came from Italy or Spain, he took advantage of a fifteen year old little girl, my little sister, I found out got pissed beyond belief, went after him and got attacked. So,he decided to make an example and turned me, ryan came to town and was acting weird so I knew what he was right away. We live here with her to help protect her but she technically swore herself to him so we can't do much there. But we are getting help. If you can't deal with that then you need to leave. We just thought that, as Kimberly's friend, you'd want to help but it seems we were wrong so go, no go on go. Go home and pretend you never heard or saw any of this. No? Ok then. Now we figure out how to tell them you're here to stay."

Ceci, Ryan, and Kim all stared at Melanie, for one thing Ceci hadn't heard her talk this much since she's been here, for another she just didn't know what to say. Finally Ryan spoke up "so are you in to help us get our humanity back and get the town back?" Suddenly Ceci found three sets of eyes turned on her, she just nodded and said "yea what the hell right?"

5

Later that night, Ceci couldn't sleep so she went downstairs to find Ryan sitting in one of the recliners. "Couldn't sleep either I see, too worked up about everything you just found out?" He smiled and Ceci noticed for the first time that he didn't have fangs. She tried to turn away fast so he wouldn't see her staring but she knew she had been caught when he chuckled. "I forgot how entertaining newbs are to this. Our fangs don't come out until we need to feed if you must know.."

She could feel herself turning red and was reaching for a subject change, anything at this point would be helpful, she thought. Then an idea struck her "so what are you guys doing exactly to help Kim? Like anything planned or" she saw him look at her sideways "what am I not trustworthy?"

He shook his head and smiled "no it's not that. Cause I mean you've already proven you are, I mean you haven't run screaming into the night so there's that. But I'm just not sure how much Kim wants you to know." She thought about that and nodded to herself more than him. Eventually she fell asleep on the couch and woke up a few hours later to voices arguing quietly. She heard Kim sounding like a mixture of scared and furious "you asked them to come here!? Why Ryan? They hate vampyres they think you guys are below them and you know that!" It took a second for Ryan but finally he said "yea they hate us, but they're raised to take care of rogue vampyres and anything else there is aren't they? This has gone on long enough, I mean aren't you tired of Jasper and his family running everything?"

Somebody walked up beside her and Ceci did her best to look asleep when the person knelt down and whispered "if you're going to live here and pretend to want to help then you better stop eavesdropping on conversations you weren't invited to. I'm not stupid I know you're awake." With that, Melanie got up and walked back to the table and Ceci, having been caught, decided to get up and join the conversation.

When she got to the table Ryan and Kim stopped arguing and looked at her "hey Ceci if you want you can sleep upstairs you don't have to st-" but Ryan cut her off "she's been listening she knows, sort of, what we're talking about and wants to help. So I suppose we should tell her." Kim looked at Ceci again this time with sadness in her eyes instead of a look of protection. Ceci looked at Ryan instead and asked "who are you calling out here? Who could possibly be able to deal with rogue vampyres?"

They all looked at each other as if seeing who would crack first, finally Ryan looked at her and said "well they're sort of like family. We've always watched out for each other, even when we weren't supposed to. They're part of a secret society called hunters of darkness or something like that. They keep track of all us 'other worlders'." Ceci looked at him for a minute "wait a minute you're making it sound like there's more than just vampyres? There's not is there?"

Ryan looked at Kim she said "whoa hey don't look at me, this is your origin story not mine." But Melanie got up and they all looked at her "get Ceci to the basement or somewhere safe they're coming to the door now." She went outside and Ryan jumped up and started shoving Ceci down the hall when Kim called to him from the living room "wait Ryan stop, false alarm!"

When they went back to the dinning room Ryan stood in front of Ceci protectively when he got a glimpse of who was at the door, he instantly relaxed and moved away.

When she went into the room she saw three boys about her age one girl around hers and Kim's age and one man standing there. There was some resemblance between the man and the girl and as she looked at the boys she saw a resemblance between them too. Siblings she thought, these

'Warriors' are just kids and he's sending his children out to deal with things that can hurt a fifteen year old girl.

Ryan was hugging the one with sandy brown hair. One of the siblings she thought she noticed they all had a haunted look in their eyes.

Ryan talked to them for a while until the one she thought was the dad took notice of Ceci standing off to the side. He smiled at her and said "I apologize for our rudeness, and for not introducing ourselves. My name is Loren this is my son Jarred, his sister Trish, that one over there, the brown hair, is Alex and the blond, is Austin." He smiled again and she lightened up a little "it's nice to meet you I'm Cecilia everyone here just calls me Ceci."

Ryan smiled encouragingly at Ceci who turned back to the man, Loren, and asked "so if I may ask, how did you become hunters or like what do you do?" At that, all the new kids stopped and looked at her. The siblings looked more and more irritated but Loren just smiled and said "we are born into it actually, it's a long story that I must hold for another time. However, I can tell you we are given weapons and blood from the Angels themselves to protect and serve our fellow brothers and sisters."

Ceci looked to Ryan who smiled and nodded at her. She took a minute to think all of this over before she looked at Loren again, then she addressed them all "ok so now we have warriors, two bad ass vampyres, and two girls who can't do much but will definitely try. What's the plan? How do we get rid of these people and revenge for what they did to Kimberly?"

6

After a few hours of milling about the house and talking more, Ceci decided not much was to be done tonight and went upstairs. As she was in her room changing for bed she heard something at her window. She walked toward it and saw a big black crow sitting there watching her, it had wings black as night that seemed to show colors as they moved its eyes though, they weren't that of a bird, or a bird Ceci had ever seen. They were nearly all black from the pupil but as she looked closer at it she saw it had blue around it like an iris. How's that possible she thought crows don't have irises, at least I've never seen one that did. She leaned closer for a better look and her bedroom door exploded open she jumped and felt instant cold air.

"Get away from the window Cecilia, that's not a normal crow!" She turned as if waking from a dream and saw Jarred standing there and he looked every bit the avenging angel she thought he should.

He crossed her room in two strides and pulled the window shut. He grabbed her by the arm and drug her out of the room into the hall. "What on God's green Earth were you thinking?" He was practically screaming at her, or at least he should've been Ceci noticed he wasn't yelling but he was furious. "You're mad at me for opening my window? It's California, it gets hot at night yes I'm going to open it?" She couldn't believe he was so worked up over a window. And everyone says I overreact, she thought. By now everyone was coming to see what the fuss was about.

Loren looked first at her calm slightly irritated self, then at Jarred who was silently brooding. "Alright Cecilia, may I ask just what happened that's irritated my son so much?" Loren asked she sighed and crossed her arms but said "honestly? I don't even know. One second I'm getting ready for bed changing, the next there's a bird at my window, and the next he's charging in and yelling at me, then just for the heck of it, he rushes me out of my room into the hallway and yells at me. So honestly, I don't know what the problem is ask him."

Loren looked slightly puzzled but nonetheless turned to Jarred expectantly not father to son Ceci realized but trainer to student. "I heard a crow's squawk and thought it was weird to hear one at this time of night, so I knocked on her door and heard something really weird like someone whispering so I chanced it and opened it. When I did I saw the birds eyes were like glowing crystalline blue and she was about to ask it in the house. Yes I yelled at her so there goes the element of surprise you can thank her for that." He finished the last part with clear anger in his voice as he glared at her.

Loren stood there staring at them for a minute before one of the other boys Austin she thought asked in a quiet voice "do you think it's her Loren?" Jarred, finally, turned his gaze to Austin and for a second she thought he was going to punch the other boy. "No I don't think it's her and I don't think you should bring it up again." He turned on his heel and left the room "ok... not that I'm complaining that he's yelling at someone else, but what was that about?" Ceci couldn't help but ask them when she saw how sad and let down they all looked.

The boy who had yet to speak finally turned to look at her " before we came here we had to fight an enemy. An enemy that.... Struck closer to home I suppose you can say." He looked to Loren who went and stood behind Trish "a few months ago we had to take down my brother-in-law he was one of the biggest enemies we've gone against to help protect everyone. He tried to get demons under his control and tried to over throw our government so he could become the ultimate and supreme ruler of us and he roped my daughter, their sister Isabelle, into it. They weren't ready for such a fight but in the end Austin was able to....put and end to it."

They all stood there while the meaning sunk in to Ceci this is what they do. They're hunters they kill. She thought, Ryan came in with a slightly-less irritated looking Jarred "well we may have an idea of how to get closer to them and figure out how to get rid of them." Kim came in with different foods for everyone "ok so we know they like blood, they need it to survive, that and not too much sun other words they'd be crispy kritters." As she was talking an idea came to Ceci "wait a minute. Didn't you say he has control of you Kim?" All eyes in the room turned to her.

She cleared her throat "well I'm not from here so I don't know all the deals going on with vampyres, but you said ever since day one he had some kind of control over you. Right? Well if he had control who's to stop him from snooping and getting her to tell him everything happening here?" Seeing where she was going to end up Melanie stepped up and took over "alright so Ceci, for once, is right he could just snoop but if there's no cause for snooping he shouldn't. He won't do much because he thinks Ryan and I are part of his group so he won't expect us to be calling hunters in." With that everyone went on talking about things Ceci had no interest in: weapons, blood, attacks, defense on and on it went.

7

"Alright guys we need to figure this out we've had sleep, Kim looks like hell, let's finish this." Jarred had walked in the kitchen a little after breakfast so everyone was a little crabby at being bossed around. Kim stood up and looked at him "what the hell does that mean? 'Kim looks like hell' screw you Jarred I'm leaving." As she went to walk out, Ryan and Melanie looked at eachother and Ceci noticed Ryan nod once and Melanie shake her head "oh my god you can read minds?" They both turned to look at her, she ducked slightly but asked the follow up questions anyway "Seriously? Have you ever spied on me?" She felt completely filled with rage but she couldn't understand why. They turned to look at her but Loren cut across them completely to answer.

"Uh actually Cecilia they can block out other minds, they only listen if they feel they need to or if it's relevant to them." Ceci turned instantly red and couldn't meet their eyes but she heard Jarred chuckling in the corner. She got up and left the room. When she went down the hallway she saw the one boy, Austin, sitting there but he had a weird blankness about his face.

"Uh you ok Austin? Do you want me to ge- ow you're hurting me Austin let go!" As she turned he reached out and grabbed her his face was blank but he started speaking "tonight is the night it happens." He said in a strange emotionless voice. "The night it happens? What are you talking about?" He didn't seem to hear her he just kept going "their worst nightmare comes to life. Unless they find the truth, don't run from destiny, this fight is yours as well." With that he dropped his head and his grip on her went completely slack. She stood there looking at him in complete fear, she realized she was shaking and trying not to cry when Alex walked in with towels. He took one look at them and jumped down the stairs to Austin.

"What did you do to him?" He almost yelled but Ceci could tell he was trying to stay calm as he examined Austin. He froze and looked at her. "What did he say? Don't lie and tell me he didn't say anything because I can tell. We're the only ones who know about this, his family, so tell me." Ceci stood for a minute thinking, when she thought she might explode she said it. "He said 'tonight is the night it happens.' Then he stopped and said 'their worst nightmare comes to life. Unless they find the truth, don't run from destiny, this fight is yours as well.'" She looked at Alex and for a minute she didn't think he'd answer. Then he said "that's not good. I know you don't understand but I do, and it's not good we need to tell them. After I make sure he's ok of course."

Once they got everyone together Ceci told them what she heard from Austin who kept looking down and wouldn't make eye contact with any of the others. When Loren finally went to him he tried to shrug away from him but Loren seemed to get through to the boy. Noticing Ceci's confusion, Ryan came over "he's part fey, which is bad, no one trusts the fey they're known liars and during the war that broke out they pledged allegiance to Chuck. The bad guy, it's a long complicated story but basically Austin feels he's bad because his blood, but Loren's always been like a dad to him since his dad Chuck, the bad guy, abandoned him. Yea I think that's it."

Ceci tried to process that along with everything else I think I'll just file all of this as what I need to know and what can be sorted through later she thought and that is definitely a later sort of thing. "Ok so we know that something's coming" said Trish "and it's somebody's worst nightmare. So we need to get this going now, it's four o'clock and we know Jaspers fed recently due to Kim's bruised up neck. I propose Jarred, or myself, go in to wherever it is they're staying and cause a problem that way we can get in and learn the place inside and out."

Ceci just stared at the girl, she was a few years younger than Cecilia herself but she was creating plans and setting them into motion in a matter of seconds. What have I gotten myself into? Ceci thought.

****

Kim stood outside the big two story house this isn't a house this is a castle she thought. I've been here hundreds if not thousands of times I can do this. As she walked to the door something in the bushes jumped out and attacked her. It pinned her to the floor and she felt something press against her throat oh my god she thought I'm going to die. Right outside of my 'sires' house. How ironic he's supposed to be my protection. As she finished the thought the door to the two story monster opened and she heard a familiar slightly accented voice call out.

"Isabelle please, is this really how we treat our guests?"

Instantly the figure got up off her and the hair on the back of Kim's neck was standing up. She rubbed her neck telling herself it's just cause you were just attacked you're ok calm down. She smiled at the man who called off the attack dog, this man who was tall, and lean with tanned skin, black hair that he always ran a hand through when I frustrated him, his movie star smile, and beautiful expensive suits he always wore. He was also her worst nightmare of all time because she knew behind that beautiful smile was a monster just waiting to be let out and set on her just as he had when she was only fifteen.

He turned to look at her as if for the first time, "ah mi amore what are you doing back here?" He asked in his slightly accented voice "I wasn't aware there was a feeding scheduled, unless you're here for something else?"She could feel her hairs on her arms and the back of her neck standing on end again as she tried to hide her fear of this man. Out of the corner of her eye she saw something shine. When she turned to look, she saw the girl had pulled out a blade similar to the ones Jarred and the others had but this one didn't glow like theirs. "Ah of course how rude of me. This is a special guest of mine who is allowed to use you as well and she's been warned not to take too much I will be the one to change you mi amore."

Kim turned to the girl and saw that she had a feral wild look to her. Her hair was black as night, her dress was-at one point- white as a newly baptized babies, and everything about her screamed run. She smiled at her and something clicked to Kim she wasn't sure what but that smile reminded her of someone. The girl smiled and said "oh she seems shell shocked. Do you normally share her Jasper?" She hadn't even finished the sentence and she moved right next to Kim and whispered the last part in her ear. Jasper saw the frightened look on Kim's face and looked at the girl they had a conversation that Kim herself couldn't hear and the girl backed off "fine I'll go check the perimeter again Jasper" she seemed to spit his name at him.

Whoa I've never seen anyone disrespect him like that and live Kim thought. He grabbed her by her arm and pulled her to him "ah mi amore when are you going to stop lying to yourself and admit you love me and the life? Hmm I know you do I can feel it when I hold you like this" he wrapped his arms around her and nuzzled her neck she instantly relaxed and moved into his arms more "when will you admit I am not the enemy?"

She sighed and turned around to look into his bright blue eyes and smiled "you know how I feel about you Jasper but you know why I have my reservations. You attacked me, all those years ago and although I have come to love you I can't be your 'princess and Queen of the world' with you. You know that you have to stop your family for what they're doing and then I will explain you to my family."

He sighed sadly and nibbled her neck making her want him even more then she could or should. When they bit you, it released an endorphin, so long as you didn't fight it the bite was truly exquisite you felt you were flying but once you fought, it hurt and burned as bad as any third degree burn. As he held her, she felt better than she had in days. She knew Jasper had started the bad guy but he had changed slowly towards her, becoming warmer than any vampyre has ever been towards his 'lunch.'

She heard a rustling and moved away from him he looked at her with eyes that seemed to be sadly amused "ya know mi amore you shouldn't have heard that any normal human wouldn't have moved." Oh god she thought am I letting him take too much? As she was thinking, he turned his attention to something over her shoulder. When she turned she saw the girl, Isabelle, standing there looking slightly amused. "It seems that my dear brother has wondered his way into town. Now how on earth could that happen if they know nothing of this town?" She said the last part looking straight at me.

"Perhaps they've heard of all the killing and blood letting near this area." Jasper said "Perhaps they don't think it's from a wild animal as the news reports say no?" He looked at her with fifty different emotions crossing his face at being interrupted. Looking at him my mind started flying through different things to ask but the one thing that came flying out was "what are you going to do?"

8

Isabelle turned towards the other girl and if looks could kill, Kim would've been killed four times over by now. Jasper looked at Kim and she knew something was wrong "I feel I've been lied to mi amore . Would you care to enlighten me or should I loose Isabelle on them?" At the look on Isabelle's face Kim knew what she had to do. Before she could answer she heard a snap of a branch and a small scream before Isabelle smiled that psychotic smile that made Kim's skin crawl. "Too late princess, the decisions been made for you."

She was gone in a flash leaving behind only a breath of wind in her place. Feeling the panic build up in her stomach and chest Kim turned to Jasper "Jasper please what's going to happen to him. Please you have to tell me please!" At the end she couldn't help but scream and when he turned she saw the look on his face and knew before he said what was going to happen. "Well mi amore it seems we have an intruder. The punishment for intruding on the royal house, as you know, is punishable by death."

As they walked in from the porch on the house Kim noticed the different people. "Why are there so many people here?" Jasper looked at her sideways but said nothing just sped up his pace. When they got to the meeting room Kim saw him, Jarred was sitting there with cuts and bruises on his face and blood running down his front. He sat there with the most uncaring or disinterested look Kim had ever seen on anyone's face who was about to be executed. He cast a bored look around the room until his eyes fell on Kim and stayed there. She felt like they were lasers drilling a hole into her then he looked down at her hand in Jasper's and froze there.

When he looked at her, it was the look of a man finding his cheating wife in bed with another. "You've got to be kidding me" was all he said. She looked at Jasper and tried to get him to understand "please Jasper please don't do this. I know you, I know you're not like this please." He pulled her hand to his lips and kissed it while looking into her eyes. He flicked his gaze to Jarred just once before he turned and left. As he went through the door she heard his voice in her head trust me mi amore I'll get him out of here.

Just then, Isabelle came out from the shadows and walked towards Jarred. His body went completely rigid and his gaze was frozen on hers. She smiled as she walked up to him, no longer the psychopath Kim noted. "Hello Jarred, dear brother, it's been a while hasn't it?"

He looked at her with the same disinterest he had as he looked around the room. Then a look of amusement lit his features "ah Izzy, it's been what? Two? Three months. Last I saw you you were a baby." She was practically snarling at him "oh and you had a stake sticking out of your chest. Course that would change anyone's appearance right?" Izzy just stood there growling at him before he finally focused on her again "so Isabelle-"

"DONT CALL ME THAT" the girl screamed Kim jumped at how angry this girl got but Jarred barely even flinched "don't call you what? The name you were born with? The name your mother and father gave you? Too many bad memories? Like I don't know... When you killed your mother!?"

Kim stepped back in complete shock of their anger, neither of them even glanced in her direction. She took one step then two back towards the door. When she finally made it to the door, they were still locked in argument. Lord I hope he's ok here with psycho was the last thing she thought as she backed out of the door.

9

Ceci and Trish were securing the perimeter on the outside of the house as the boys were making their way in. Loren was talking to them via the ear piece each of them was wearing, Melanie and Ryan were our scouts seeing as how they were already inside. Who would've thought being a vampyre would've come in handy for this mission? She thought.

 "Ok everybody just remember Jarred was the bait, which they took gratefully and willingly." Loren came over the ear piece. Ceci turned to look at Trish how did somebody who's no older then me, maybe even younger, get into this lifestyle? She thought as the other girl sat there holding her blade with her mouth as she fixed her hair. "Do you really think it's smart to put that in your little blade holder before you do your hair? Aren't you afraid of getting cut or something?" Ceci couldn't help but ask, Trish smiled but right as she went to answer, Cecilia heard Ryan's voice come in her head.

Watch yourself Cecilia we haven't seen jarred in sometime, this isn't your fight. Let them take it from here. Just as soon as it was there it was gone. What the hell? She thought who the hell is he to tell me when to stay and when to run? Trish turned to her "ok Ceci we're going in, I'm not gonna lie to you. Something went wrong we have no contact with jarred but the last thing we heard from him was that Kim isn't in as much trouble as we thought." She grabbed one of her blades and handed it to Ceci "these are special blades enchanted with the magic of the fey anyone or anything gets in your way? Cut it down."

With that she stood and started going down the hill into what could be Ceci's first and last battle. Here goes nothing she thought and headed down quickly falling in step with the other girl.

10

"Damn it" Ryan said as he slammed his fist down on the table. Melanie raised her eyebrow at him as she got a drink from her glass "something wrong?" She asked, he had his head down and was leaning over the table barely able to hide his irritation with the new girl Cecilia. Why won't she listen? He thought why is she so damned stubborn? "Ceci is being ridiculous." Was all he said but he knew by the look Melanie gave him she got what he was saying.

The song playing through the palace came to a halt. Melanie looked at Ryan and her face perfectly mirrored his thoughts something's wrong.

They looked up at the top of the twin winding staircase in the foyer to see Jasper's brother Stephan standing with his arms open wide addressing the crowd. "Ah mi amores we are so glad all the children of the night can make it." He waited for the applause to die down before continuing.

"Tonight is a special night, not just for us but for the entire coven of night children!" Ryan looked at Melanie and saw her face exactly mirrored what he was thinking not good. Stephan turned around and motioned for someone to come forward. Ryan took his chance to quickly look around the room and saw the others slowly forming a perimeter around the room good they were able to get in at least somethings gone right. He thought.

When he glanced at Melanie he saw her do the same thing and heard her in his mind I have a bad feeling about this. He nodded for her to continue Stephan never throws parties just cause, and if its 'for the good of all of the nights children' that means it's bad for everyone else. He nodded again to let her know he heard but said nothing else instead he thought to himself where the hell is Jarred at? He should've been down here by now or we should've heard something.

Just then, the doors behind Stephan opened and two guards stepped through bowing low. "My friends, I give you the newest to our clan. Isabell Luisella Ottavia Princess of the night children." Ryan didn't need to look around the room to have his fears confirmed he knew without a doubt every single one of his friends there had all gone completely pale at this news.

The girl, Isabell, stood there towering over them, looking down at what was now 'her subjects.' She stood in a brand new completely stunning dress. A bridal gown Ryan realized. He turned and looked at Melanie for confirmation but her eyes were still stuck to the scene unrolling before them. It wasn't a wedding gown per-say, but it was definitely designed off the idea of one, completely white with a stunning bejeweled bodice and an intricately designed veil woven just as intricately into her hair which was black as night. She stood there for a moment longer before she moved to address the crowd who was waiting with bated breath.

  "My brothers and sisters I'm humbled to be welcomed into such an elite coven. I will do anything in my power to keep the good name Otavia as grand and regal as it should be. And if anyone so dares to stand against us I will do all in my power to not only end them but wipe their entire family and it's pitiful history out of existence." As the crowd broke into cheers Ryan turned to look at Melanie who was just as shocked as he was. When he flicked his eyes up to see if the others were still in place he saw that Austin had gone from his normal pale appearance to what could've been mistaken for the paleness any of his neighbors standing by him had.

This is even worse than we thought was all he could muster to Melanie.

****

Ok so rather than being inside in a room full of vampyres I'm walking around their house or I'm sitting behind a tree. Not exactly how I pictured my first mission to go. "Ok Ceci we haven't heard anything from anyone" said Trish "so I'm growing a little anxious.. If you could imagine me more anxious." She smiled slightly at the other girl and paced a little "on my round I saw the one brother-Stephan I think- speaking to the room but I didn't see much after that." She plopped down beside Ceci on the ground.

"Sometimes I wish they'd include me on the big stuff instead of treating me like a baby or their little sister."

The silence sat between them for a while just building, the tension was getting thick enough to cut with a knife "Honestly I don't know how you do it." Said Ceci finally cracking first. Trish turned to look at her but suddenly shot up and stood rigid as a board. Feeling and seeing the tension Ceci got up too and waited tense and ready for the battle that was sure to be coming.

When nothing happened right away, though, she looked at the other girl who had gone completely still and white "Trish what's wrong? Are you ok what is it?" When the other girl didn't answer right away she touched her shoulder making the other girl jump. "Oh Ceci this is bad really bad. Badder than we thought."

Ceci turned to look at the mansion not quite understanding what was just 'so bad' when the other girl turned to her. "Look remember when we told you about our sister? And some bad stuff happened with her?" She looked at Ceci expectantly "yea" she said "but I also remember you didn't tell me everything you said 'I didn't need to know' or something."

Trish sat there considering this before she said "ok fine screw up on our part sue us. Long story short, she helped in getting our mother annihilated, when the time came to choose sides she chose the bad side, we went against her and Chuck-the baddest of the bad guy- and it was a fight between her and Jarred. They were dead locked when Austin came up and it was a choice between letting her live, and Jarred dying or Jarred- I think you can guess who he chose."

She glanced at Ceci to make sure the other girl followed before continuing "Austin staked her an-" "wait a minute." Said Ceci cutting her of much to the other girls annoyance "why would he stake her? Was she a vampyre?" "No she wasn't I guess you get points for paying attention though, she was bad he had no more weapons save for a stake.. I don't know about you but I'm pretty sure a stake would kill anyone human or vampyre alike. Anyways he staked her and that was that. Or so we thought."

They both stood there for a moment before Ceci finally realized Trish didn't finish what she was saying before "ok so she wasn't a vampyre but she is dead." She turned to look at the girl "she is dead isn't she?" Trish took a deep breath before answering "well there's something you need to know. Vampyres are created many different ways, I mean sure the movies have hit on the typical way." She started counting them off on her hand " being bit from one-duh-, them giving you their blood(again duh), however there are a bunch of other ways."

Ceci looked at her completely shocked "ok" she said slowly "but what does that have todo-" Trish cut her off "with why I'm freakin out? Yea I'm getting to that. But you need to know the basics ok? Now then so you know typical ways but there are others, such as-" she started ticking them off on her fingers again " first they can change you over time-like Jasper was with Kim- second, this ones by far the most painful too, they can change you simultaneously over a small course of time. Only problem is it takes three elders or four(or more) young vampyres and they bite you one after the other for like a day or two and it's not pleasurable at all. It's the most painful thing you'll ever experience in your life it's like something is tearing through you threatening to tear you apart completely. That's why it's not usually used it typically kills the person. And finally there's the fact that some are born one."

Ceci was completely shocked by that and could only stare "yea it's rare but it does happen. I'm telling you this because you need to know what you're up against. Now back to why I was freaking out before? Jasper's brother-Stephan- brought out his newest prodigy for all the night's children to see; he called her his princess. When she came out, Ryan told me it got worse then we can imagine. Can you take a guess as to who it was?"

Ceci sat there for a moment absorbing everything she was just told *why do they do this to me?* She thought *they spring all this information on me and expect me to be completely fine with it. Take it in stride.* As she asked that last question, another voice came in her head this one deeper than her own *because you're a warrior now you are one of them. When you said you'd help Kim they accepted you to their ranks.* She looked at Trish who was standing still, for once, looking down expectantly "it's your sister isn't it? Isabelle?"

Trish finally sat down almost defeated "yea it is. I'm sure even you can see, or guess, how bad this is? Which is why" she said as she stood back up and dusted herself off "you need to go back, you've done more than anyone of us could have asked. I know you hate this but you need to know, this isn't your fight go back help my father with coordinating or something. Kim would absolutely hate and kill me if you got hurt on my watch."

Ceci couldn't help but agree with all of what she said she wasn't a warrior she didn't belong in this world at also when Trish pushed her back to the path and told her how far to go and where, to get back to the base of operations she didn't argue but actually went. *Alright now if only I don't get lost* she thought. As she got further from Trish and closer to camp she felt better and better until something black lunged at her from the side of the trail. She tried to fight it but it was too fast for her uncoordinated senses to fully see. She struck out like Jarred had tried to teach her and connected with something "OW" she screamed when she pulled her hand back it throbbed. But she kept trying to fend it off when she thought she could get away she took her chance. She faked left and hit right, again feeling the throbbing pain, and took her chance to run. Only she didn't get far before what she was fighting with, lunged out from behind her and hit her upside the head. She had just enough time to think how badly this was gonna hurt before everything around her went black.

11

Ok I've got to get out of here thought Kim when she got out of the room with Jarred and Izzy. I've been to this house thousands of times, how is it even possible to get lost? She asked herself for what seemed like the thousandth time. She turned the corner and ran right into Stephan who looked surprised to see her and then irritated that she spilled his drink on him. "Ah," he said "my brothers little play thing. What are you doing wandering these halls all alone? Aren't you afraid that an actual vampyre will find you and take you?" He said and smiled at her showing all of his teeth even his fangs.

   She shuddered and started to back away babbling out the quickest excuse she could think "well I uh that is Jasper sent me to get something for him but I kind of got lost so, if ya don't mind I'm gonna-" as she turned around, she again ran into a person this time thankfully it wasn't Stephan.

When she looked up she saw to her horror it wasn't Jasper either but Stephan's lackeys. "Sorry princess but my dear brother isn't going to save you this time, and besides the penalty for wandering this house is punishable by death or, ya know, death." He smiled as he watched the color drain from her face he turned on his heel and the guards holding her, drug her kicking and fighting after him.

When they got to a set of big gold-looking doors Stephan stopped and went to the other room. These doors lead to the foyer she realized as she was gonna try to take a step Stephan rematerialized in front of her.

"We have a grand announcement to make." He said enjoying how he made her jump at his appearance. "You will be brought in at the end and you will be used as we want whether she decides to change you for my sad little brother or kill you is up to her." The door opened and out came "oh lord no, not psychopath." Kim couldn't help but say it and she instantly regretted it when the girl smacked her so hard she swore she could see stars. She went to hit her again when Stephan grabbed her arm "uh-uh my princess leave her, you never want bruised food." He dropped her arm to the side and when he went through the door she stood there next to Kim. When Stephan came back for her she whispered just barely loud enough to for Kim to hear "you die first little girl."

With that, she walked through the doors the guards stayed put never once budging. After a few minutes the doors opened again and Stephan nodded to the two guards, they drug her trough the door and onto the grand staircase looking down at a crowd of vampyres. Great I knew I was walking into the den but come on she thought.

When she looked into the crowd she saw her friends Melanie and Ryan but as Kim looked into the crowd more, she saw the rest of them unbelievable she thought. Stephan came towards her and jerked her away from the two guards holding her tightly he pushed her down on her knees in front of all of them.

"And now, we see the beginning of a long reign of our soon-to-be-Queen." Isabelle came up to Kim and looked down on her "what a joke." She said, "this? This is what he was going to give life to? He was going to awaken her?" As she said it she picked up the other girl and held her by the shirt "she doesn't deserve the offer."

With that she sank her teeth into the other girls neck and began drinking deeply it stung worse than ever before. Oh my god I'm really going to die she thought she forced her eyes open and looked out in the crowd and saw what Stephan was too busy to see. The guys! She thought they're coming!

As Isabelle drank more and more Kim felt her life draining from her, when all of a sudden the doors behind them blew open with enough force to throw the two girls into the rail of the stairs and tear Izzy's teeth from the other girls neck; causing Kim to cry out in pain. She looked up groggily and saw to her surprise Jasper, and he was mad.

Not just his regular irritated look he'd have when dealing with his brother but completely pissed off. Oh great was the last thing she thought before she passed out.

Ryan stood in the crowd as Isabelle went for Kim he couldn't move damn it! He thought I'm stuck here can't go against them yet can't just stand here. He was trapped a vampyre and trapped how ridiculous even as he thought it he saw the others start moving into action. Slowly, quietly, and quickly taking out anything and everything in their way. Austin, having regained his composure, nodded once sharply to Ryan and moved forward.

As they moved through the crowd like shadows Ryan couldn't help but think, the doors burst open and Kim was thrown away from Isabelle. They bounced off the railing of the stairs Ryan saw Melanie wince from the corner of his eye. "We will get to her Melanie we will save her" she nodded and stayed where she was.

Come on Kim move he thought. When he tore his gaze away from the too-still Kim he saw the reason they were thrown away. It was Jasper, and he was mad he took everything in in just a quick glance and launched himself at his brother. The two of them fought each other moving too fast for any human eye to follow but not quite fast enough to get past the hunters. Austin had made his way to the top of the stairs and started squaring up his opponent: Isabelle.

Ryan followed Melanie and watched her back for anyone that would come to attack her. He took out a man who was dressed as if from the nineteenth century and a woman whom he knows had just recently been awakened. As they went up the stairs slowly they heard more and more thuds and cries in the crowd. He gave a brief glance and saw Trish had come inside and was holding her own fighting these creatures. She was being circled by two or three as one went to attack she deftly dodged away and swept out kicking another effectively knocking its feet out from under it. She pinned the vampyre to the ground and staked them then went for the other two quickly finishing them off as well.

When they finally got to the top of the stairs they saw Austin locked in a deadly dance. Isabelle struck out but Austin was too fast she snarled in frustration and kept trying to hit him. Melanie went straight for Kim kneeling beside her looking her over for the worst of her injuries. "We have to get her out of here." She said looking at Ryan trying not to cry she's bad Ryan really bad I don't know if we can fix this without changing her. She thought to him what she couldn't say aloud.

He nodded and started to help lift her when someone else came through the doors, Ryan stood protectively in front of the girls he thought of as family great what now he thought. As he went on defensive ready to take out anyone, or anything, that came through the door but right as he went to attack he realized he knew the person. Bruised and bloody here or there from battles or whatever happened after he was taken shown clearly in his face and neck but through that Ryan could tell it was Jarred.

"Well it's about damn time!" Ryan couldn't help but smile at the other guy the moment of happiness at seeing him alive was short lived when he looked past Ryan to where Melanie was with Kim "what the hell happened to her!?"

  "Look right now, it doesn't matter Austin is taking care of it." Jarred looked at Ryan and nodded "he needs this but he can't do it alone." Jarred went up to Melanie and Kim he knelt down and looked at her "she is going to be ok right?" Melanie nodded and Jarred stood "ok look I know how to get you out but Austin needs help. He had to go against her once and it practically killed him to do it, she's much stronger this time we can't leave him."

Ryan picked Kim up from where she lay unconscious in front of Melanie, "come on let's get her out of here and to Loren."

12

Trish was cutting her way through the crowd of vampyres up to the stairs, they were confused and angry at the sudden ambush. She fought as best she could getting cuts and scrapes here and there. She finally was able to get to Alex who was firing arrows as fast as he could. She saw a young- newly awakened- vampyre start charging Alex's back so she threw one of her blades which landed straight in the middle of the vampyre's chest and made her singe and disappear.

"Nice one, good to see the student almost surpass the teacher." He said with a smile "yea yea you can congratulate me for my awesomeness later. Right now, we need to figure out how to get to Austin he needs us." She jerked her head up towards the stairs where Austin and Izzy were fighting, he was doing great at defense but that was all he was doing: defense.

"Damn it" said Alex "I knew this was bad." He shot down the last vampyre that was near them and hurried up the stairs. He shot an arrow and hit not Izzy but Jasper as he and Stephan went by "well not who I was aiming for but....." he shrugged his shoulders "seems just as good as any." He joked but when he turned back Izzy kicked out at Austin and sent him tumbling down the stairs into Alex. Trish jumped out of the way before they took her down too.

"Oh look who's decided to come play with the big kids." Said Izzy "are you ok without daddy holding your hand?" She asked mockingly, Trish didn't answer she just took her blade out and stood ready to attack. Izzy just laughed "you can't possibly think that you out of everyone here" she motioned around the room "can take me down? You're just a kid who has pent up anger and no training you couldn't hurt a fl- AHH" she screamed as something shot past Trish's head and hit the other girl in the right shoulder.

Trish looked at Isabelle and saw an arrow sticking out of her shoulder before the other girl ripped it out. "That hurt pretty boy, I was wrong earlier you die first." She came at them all fun and games forgotten she attacked as fast and hard as she could hitting and scratching them. This is it she thought I'm really going to die tonight at the hand of my sister.

  Austin and Alex circled her one on either side completely distracting her. Trish she heard the slightly accented voice say her name in her head. She turned to look and saw a bloodied Jasper standing there. Instantly she went on defensive he held his hands up in surrender "I am not against you I know you have no proof but I swear I do not condone what my brother has done please let me help you."

  She turned helplessly to Alex and Austin but they were still busy keeping Isabell's attention. "You expect me to just trust you?" She asked incredulously "after everything you and your family has done to Kim and her family, this town, hell even my family?" He stood there and she saw something change in him, no longer was he the cocky and cold vampyre she'd seen since she got here. Now she saw a defeated man standing here looking hurt and betrayed and wanting to prove himself. She sighed "if I trust you and you betray us know I will hunt you down and destroy you myself."

He chuckled at her and said "ok you have my word if I betray you, you can kill me. Anyways I can help you take her out." He nodded towards Isabelle who was gaining the upper hand on the two guys. "Ok fine, tell me what to do now." He assessed the problem a little more before finally nodding "his arrows, they're made of silver yes?" At that Trish nodded "yea all our weapons are silver and blessed by the Angel herself."

He nodded "ok give me one of your blades and when they-" he motioned to Austin and Alex "go on either side of your sister go in front of her, turn her around, and get her back so it faces me I will hit her from behind and when the initial shock hits, hit her again in the front, she's young, she's strong, she was created by elders, but she's not completely invincible. Two, or more, blessed blades in her? She's gone."

Trish nodded and handed him the small dagger she had from her boot and gave it to him, he laughed and said "only a beautiful woman could pull off such a deadly move so flawlessly." She snatched her hand back "and only a disgusting pedophile would would go after a child," she snapped after that she turned around and went toward the boys.

As she got there she noticed that they were losing the battle pretty badly. She came up and drew Isabelle's attention she hit her with a kick to the leg making Izzy stop her attack on Alex. "You wanna act like a big girl?" She asked "fine I'll treat you like one little sister." She spat and lunged at Trish giving her a split second to react. One clawed hand raked down her left shoulder leaving three huge gashes all the way down "AH!" Cried Trish she threw her blades up defending herself and turning at the same time.

Isabelle followed Trish's lead too busy attacking to see that Jasper was closing in on her lining up his strike. Isabelle punched the other girl in the side of the head so hard making her drop to the floor seeing stars. She pulled her foot back to kick her once, twice, and then Alex stepped in front of her dragging a dagger across Izzy's face making her howl in pain and step back right at the same time Jasper struck.

The girls eyes went wide as shock registered she clutched at her chest and kept trying to fight but somethings changed Trish thought she's not fighting us then realization hit she's fighting not to get to them but to get away from them.

Isabelle was fighting desperately now but she was infinitely weaker than before. Trish and Alex fought her while Austin got the stake ready, when he had it poised Isabelle kicked out and knocked out Trish's legs from under her making him miss. Trish got up and fought with renewed energy come on she thought just a little more "get the arms!" Trish turned and saw Austin hand the stake to Jasper who had yelled the command at them. Of course! He's faster and stronger he'll nail it first try!

Trish ran with Alex to pin the arms but couldn't hold Izzy with her arm as bad as it was Austin was there by her side in an instant to help. Once they had her pinned, Jasper came up. Seeing him, Izzy smiled "ah brother I'm glad you're here," she said weakly. "Do you see what these little pests are doing to me?" Jasper smiled "always thinking we're better" he stepped towards her "don't worry mi amore I'll help you get away from them." He stroked the side of her face making her sag in relief, but as he pulled the stake out she tensed "what are you-" she couldn't finish Jasper lunged forward shoving the stake in her chest. Her eyes went wide in shock at being betrayed by her 'brother'

He motioned for Alex and Austin to let go. They stood there a little longer before doing so and stepped back. Austin looked up and saw Trish leaning against the wall, he started to run over right as she slid down the wall landing on the floor roughly. She had gone completely pale and clammy and had started to breathe raggedly.

He rushed over to her side "Trish! Are you ok? Alex!" he called "get me something to wrap her arm get me the healing dagger." Alex was beside him in no time he handed it over and Austin started drawing out the rune that would heal. Only it wasn't working. Black spots were starting to cover her vision, she looked up as Jasper came between them "you need to wrap her arm as best you can, use this" he said as he handed them part of the sweater Izzy had been wearing. Austin grimaced but took it and started wrapping.

Alex jumped up immediately "why aren't the runes working vampyre?" Trish held up a hand and started to answer in a low whispered voice "it's because the wound is too great you need to get me to my father he can help." "Of course he will," said Austin she felt someone scoop her up and then the world went black as she past out.

13

"Ok Ryan good news," said Jarred coming out from the house. "They won't be back to this place, everything's set in place my fathers brought some of the members of the conclave so they've allowed us to burn this place down. Not only to get rid of the lure it brings to humans to come in here and 'investigate' but also so none of the bodies can be found."

As he said this, Ryan could see flames in some of the windows. He shook his head but smiled "you got a little soot on your face bro, Kim's doing better by the way." They had brought her out to where Loren and the rest had been waiting everyone was here except "wait a minute where's Cecilia?"

Loren looked at Ryan for the first time since they brought in Kim "she was with Trish when she went in we figured Cecilia did as well." He paused "she's not with you?" Ryan shook his head he went to the other room where Trish was just waking up. Austin blocked his way "no, just whatever you have to say or ask no. She's healing and doesn't need anymore stress let her get better."

He turned on his heel and stormed out of the room Ryan looked at Austin to ask him something when Alex broke the silence "Kim." He said, they both turned to him questioningly "she needs to know that Ceci isn't here. I'll break the news if you want." As he started to walk towards the door Melanie appeared in the doorway "no" she said, "Ryan and I should do it. We're her family." She looked at Ryan who took a moment to move "she's right guys" they walked out and Melanie stopped him "where's Jarred at he should be there too?"

"He stormed out earlier when he couldn't question Trish I'm honestly not sure where he went probably upstairs training again." Said Austin, they both looked up for a second before moving down the hall. When they got in the room they saw Kim was sitting up and talking to Loren, when Melanie and Ryan came in they looked up and Kim smiled "hey!"

Melanie went right over and hugged her Ryan stepped out with Loren who turned to him "don't worry it's not my place to tell her anything about Cecilia but I beg you tell her soon. The longer she doesn't know the worse it will be." He patted Ryan on the back before leaving. As he turned the corner he called "don't worry I'll talk to Jarred as well." With that, Ryan went back in and shut he door behind him. Kim was laughing and talking to Melanie "God," she said "I can't believe that after all of the training and fighting and everything, I'm still taken out by," she paused "a banister a freaking banister."

She looked at both of them and put her head down in shame "Ceci's gonna laugh at me, isn't she?" When she looked back up at them she saw the worry written in both of their faces. Instantly she shot up "what is it?" She demanded Melanie pushed her back on the bed "calm down jumping up and into battle isn't going to help anyone least of all yourself so cool it." She told her "and about Ceci..." She trailed off looking at Ryan for help.

"Come on! Don't do that to me! Just tell me." Kim threw her hands up in exasperation just as someone said "she's gone we don't know where she is we've lost her." Ryan turned to see Jarred standing in the doorway with his arms across his chest "figured we could get it out there ya know, stop stalling." He turned back to Kim and saw there were tears in her eyes. "Don't worry we'll get her back we've got people looking for her ev-" "how can you find her though!? You don't even know where she is!" Kim was frantic now Jarred pushed past Melanie and sat on the bed with Kim he pulled her to him and hugged her.

Ryan, completely shocked turned to Melanie and saw her eyebrows shoot up in surprise Jarred looked at them "shut up." Kim smiled and finally calmed down, Jarred stood up "if you're ok," he said to Kim "and if you don't decide to kill me in the next five seconds," he said to Melanie and Ryan "I'm gonna go check my sister and help my father look for Cecilia." Kim nodded and he hesitated but kissed her forehead before practically running out the door.

Melanie turned to her sister "what the f-" Ryan cut her off "we don't have time" she looked at him like she was gonna kill him "trust me I get it," he said hastily " but we have to find Ceci that's most important: find her now, kill her" he looked towards Kim "later. Deal?" It took a few moments for Melanie to nod in agreement "fine." She said Kim got up "ok my side life aside, let's get on this. Where was she last seen."

They went back towards Trish's room but found no one was in there *I seriously wish they would tell us when they did stuff like that* Melanie sent Ryan. He nodded in agreement but didn't say anything. They turned back around and went to the study there they found everyone pouring over what looked like a music box.

Jarred looked up and smiled at Kim but ducked when he caught Melanie looking at him *memo to me* Ryan heard *kill him later* he smiled at Melanie and nodded. Loren saw the look given to his son and turned to them "I'm glad to see Kimberly has made such a good recovery," he said Kim saw Trish and couldn't help herself "what happened to Ceci?" Trish looked at them and shook her head, she went to shrug but couldn't. Her arm had been healed mostly but still needed a sling, "honestly? I don't know, when you guys said you saw Izzy in there I told her this wasn't her fight. I told her she needs to go back to the base camp thing and wait it out with my father. Last I saw her she was heading this way but when I woke up they said she never made it. And to make it even more weird, this box was delivered today but none of us could get it opened."

Ryan looked at Melanie to see if she knew and was a little surprised to see her looking at it as if it held the answers to the universe. "What is it?" He asked she turned to him to answer but Kim took one look at it and instantly tears sprang to her eyes. "What's wrong?" Ryan asked it took a moment but Melanie found her voice, "that" she started groggily she cleared her throat "that's our sisters music box from when we were kids." Ryan was floored their sister? They haven't talked to or about her in years.

  Loren thought this over, "why would your sister send you an old music box?" Melanie looked to her younger sister who shook her head "we don't know." Kim reached for the box again, this time no one stopped her. When she touched it a shimmering yellow light flashed through the room and the lid opened.

"What the hell was that?" Asked Jarred he took a step closer to Kim almost protectively. Kim looked down into the box and her breath caught "oh no" was all she said Ryan and Melanie moved as one to stand behind her pushing Jarred out of the way. Ryan reached in the box and pulled out a letter and a lock of hair.

"You think you've won? That was just a minor victory compared to what's to come. You may have won the battle but I guarantee, you will loose the war mi amores"

Ryan looked around the room at everyone after reading the note the look was the same: fear, regret, anger, and most of all confusion. "What is he talking about 'its about to get worse'?" Austin asked "Jasper got rid of his biggest threat how can there be something else?" He looked around at the group who had nothing to say except when Kim picked up the lock of hair, the hair on the back of Ryan's neck stood up "I don't know but I can guarantee you this, this is Cecilia's hair, and if they do have her then this is going to get harder. It's not over and I guarantee Ceci isn't the only person they've kidnapped."

"Well," said Jarred "who's up for a road trip?"

The next few pages are an excerpt from the upcoming title to this series, Betrayed.

My name is Kimberly, and I'm just your typical 18 year old girl, crashing parties and meeting new people here or there. My family is pretty typical, two sisters(one I never talked to until kind of recently) a mom and a dad. My sister Melanie is about what you'd expect from a typical older sister with the added bonus of being a vampyre.. Yup you heard that right she's a vampyre, course no one knows how she became one she just showed up one day like that. I mean there are a few different ways you can be turned of course. First dear old Dracula can come in the night and bite you gifting you with his blood(if he really likes you and feels like keeping you around for five or six more centuries,) next there's the whole painful way of having two or three elders feed of you for a few days all while injecting you with blood and hoping that your body accepts the change(that way is the way to make strong 'new ones'), and a whole bunch of other ways I don't feel like getting into right now.
Anyways so my friends and I(they're like these warrior descendants from angels or demons? I'm not sure which anymore) have been searching round the clock for my friend Cecilia she came out here to live with us after her mom passed away her aunt thought it would be good for her to be with friends.... Yea she was having a good time until everything that happened with me and my past and what's really going on with this

town came out.

Oh yea that reminds me, so our town-good ol' Lake Elsinore in California-was just your typical average town, until of course this family came to town. They were nice: prim, proper from out of country, had the whole foreign thing going for them. Until of course it turned out that they were some super old and powerful vampyre family bent on enslaving the world one small town at a time. One of their sons decided to take a liking to me (which by the way is another way a vampyre can be made). His name is Jasper and oddly enough he's actually become part of our group of friends. He had decided to make me one of his 'changelings' basically glorified food that may, or most likely may not, get turned into a vampyre one day. They feed off of you using you like a lunch box giving you some of their blood until eventually you get enough to become a vampyre. Slowly but surely he was doing this to me until everything went to hell. His brother, Stephan, decided to take everything into his own hands and brought in an even bigger psychopath. Her name was Isabelle and she was awakened by Stephan and a few elders through that seriously painful process(ouch).

So anyways through all that our friends (the elite warriors) came to town to help us get rid of Jasper and his family. Jasper turned out to actually hate what his family was doing to us and everyone else they hurt so he became like a spy working with us and his family. When everything came out he chose to side with us

and helped us take down Isabelle.
When all that was said and done we realized Cecilia was missing and have been working round the clock to try and find her. We had one lead which turned out to be an old music box and a strand of hair. Weird right?
"Kim hello anyone in there?" Jarred stood In front of me waving his hands to get your attention "what? What I'm here! Get your hands out of my face!"

He laughed "you have no idea what I asked do you?" I rolled my eyes at him "look I was thinking about something ok? Now did you find something or? I mean we can have Jasper look again maybe?" I said throwing a big smile and batting my eyelashes at my old 'sire' he smiled at me "no señorita I must admit that even I haven't found anything yet."
Jasper used to be the bad guy I guess you could say he went after me when they came to town. Since then, he's turned a new leaf and is currently helping us try to find Ceci. "Any ideas how to find her?" Trish asked walking in eating a Popsicle I turned and looked at her "aw come on you know I'm allergic to pomegranate! No, nothing yet sadly though I did kind of have an idea, but I was waiting to check with Melanie first." Trish thought about that for about, oh I don't know, two seconds and said "no need just tell us we'll decide."
"Really? What kind of team work is that dear Trish?" Said Ryan as he walked in with Melanie. Jarred turned and ducked slightly before quickly going back to the first thing he could get his hands on. Oh lord

he's still scared of my sister. What did she tell him? I looked at Trish who had momentarily looked embarrassed before saying "it's the kind of team work that gets the job done. You'd know that, if you'd let Kim be one of us." I shot an incredulous look at Ryan and Melanie before turning to Trish "look I'm not sure where exactly that came from but stop. We're all on the same team ok? we can't sit here and fight eachother that's exactly what Stephan wants."

Clapping sounded from the back of the room and I looked to see Jasper clapping. I gave him my best stop just stop look before turning back to them. But Jasper still spoke "ok I do agree with Kim Stephan wants to break us apart and he'll take it anyway he can. So what do we do?" I looked back at the box and Ceci's hair and thought about it "alright look Melanie I've been thinking." I looked up to see Melanie and Ryan looking at me expectantly I took a deep breath before continuing. "Well we found that box right? It's pointing to Melissa. Although how Melissa got tied into this, I'll never know I think that we need to go to Melissa.... See if she can help in anyway."

Made in the USA
Lexington, KY
17 February 2017